My Emotions
ANGRY

A Crabtree Roots Book

AMY CULLIFORD

CRABTREE
Publishing Company
www.crabtreebooks.com

School-to-Home Support for Caregivers and Teachers

This book helps children grow by letting them practice reading. Here are a few guiding questions to help the reader with building his or her comprehension skills. Possible answers appear here in red.

Before Reading:

- What do I think this book is about?
  - *This book is about feeling angry.*
  - *This book is about what feeling angry looks or feels like.*

- What do I want to learn about this topic?
  - *I want to learn what to do if I feel angry.*
  - *I want to learn what feeling angry looks like.*

During Reading:

- I wonder why...
  - *I wonder why we yell when we are angry.*
  - *I wonder why we frown when we are angry.*

- What have I learned so far?
  - *I have learned that angry is an emotion.*
  - *I have learned drawing can help when you are angry.*

After Reading:

- What details did I learn about this topic?
  - *I have learned that it is okay to be angry.*
  - *I have learned that there are many ways you can cool down after being angry.*

- Read the book again and look for the vocabulary words.
  - *I see the word* ***vegetables*** *on page 4 and the word* ***yell*** *on page 7. The other vocabulary words are found on page 14.*

What makes me **angry**?

I am angry when I eat **vegetables**.

I **yell** when I am angry.

I am angry when
no one can play.

I **frown** when I am angry.

What can I do when
I am angry?

I can **draw** a picture.

I can go ride my **bike**.

Word List

Sight Words

a
am
can
eat
go
I
makes
me
my
no
one
what
when

Words to Know

angry

bike

draw

frown

vegetables

yell

50 Words

What makes me **angry**?

I am angry when I eat **vegetables**.

I **yell** when I am angry.

I am angry when no one can play.

I **frown** when I am angry.

What can I do when I am angry?

I can **draw** a picture.

I can go ride my **bike**.

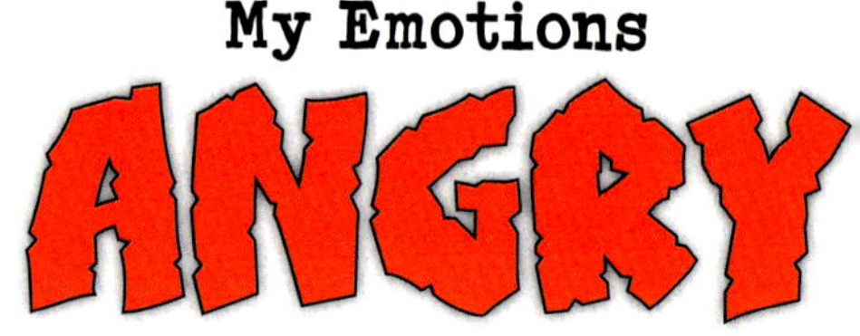

Written by: Amy Culliford
Designed by: Rhea Wallace
Series Development: James Earley
Proofreader: Ellen Rodger
Educational Consultant: Marie Lemke M.Ed.

Photographs:
Shutterstock: Juan Pablo Gonzaález: cover; maxim ibragimov: p. 1; TY Lim: p. 3, 14; thevisualsyou need: p. 5, 14; wavebreakmedia: p. 6, 14; Olga Enger: p. 8-9, 14; Mandy Godbehear: p. 10; Julia Kuzhetsova: p. 11, 14; Spotmatik Ltd: p. 13, 14

Library and Archives Canada Cataloguing in Publication

Title: Angry / Amy Culliford.
Names: Culliford, Amy, 1992- author.
Description: Series statement: My emotions | "A Crabtree roots book".
Identifiers: Canadiana (print) 20210156694 | Canadiana (ebook) 20210156708 | ISBN 9781427139627 (hardcover) | ISBN 9781427139689 (softcover) | ISBN 9781427133380 (HTML) | ISBN 9781427139740 (read-along ebook) | ISBN 9781427133984 (EPUB)
Subjects: LCSH: Anger in children—Juvenile literature. | LCSH: Anger—Juvenile literature.
Classification: LCC BF723.A4 C85 2021 | DDC j152.4/7—dc23

Library of Congress Cataloging-in-Publication Data

Names: Culliford, Amy, 1992- author.
Title: Angry / Amy Culliford.
Description: New York : Crabtree Publishing, 2021. | Series: My emotions, a crabtree roots book | Includes index.
Identifiers: LCCN 2021009523 (print) | LCCN 2021009524 (ebook) | ISBN 9781427139627 (hardcover) | ISBN 9781427139689 (paperback) | ISBN 9781427133380 (ebook) | ISBN 9781427133984 (epub) | ISBN 9781427139740 (read along)
Subjects: LCSH: Anger in children--Juvenile literature. | Anger--Juvenile literature. | Emotions in children--Juvenile literature.
Classification: LCC BF723.A4 C85 2021 (print) | LCC BF723.A4 (ebook) | DDC 155.4/1247--dc23
LC record available at https://lccn.loc.gov/2021009523
LC ebook record available at https://lccn.loc.gov/2021009524

Crabtree Publishing Company
www.crabtreebooks.com 1-800-387-7650

Printed in Canada/092022/CPC20220913

 In Canada: We acknowledge the financial support of the Government of Canada through the Canada Book Fund for our publishing activities.

Published in the United States
Crabtree Publishing
347 Fifth Avenue, Suite 1402-145
New York, NY, 10016

Published in Canada
Crabtree Publishing
616 Welland Ave.
St. Catharines, Ontario L2M 5V6